FAIRY TALES GONE BAD
FRANKENSTILTSKIN

By

Joseph Coelho

Illustrated by

Freya Hartas

WALKER
BOOKS

First published in Great Britain 2021 by Walker Books Ltd
87 Vauxhall Walk, London SE11 5HJ

2 4 6 8 10 9 7 5 3 1

Text © 2021 Joseph Coelho
Illustrations © 2021 Freya Hartas

The right of Joseph Coelho and Freya Hartas to be identified as author and
illustrator respectively of this work has been asserted by them in accordance
with the Copyright, Designs and Patents Act 1988

This book has been typeset in Archer

Printed and bound in China

British Library Cataloguing in Publication Data:
a catalogue record for this book is available from the British Library

ISBN 978-1-4063-8967-8

www.walker.co.uk

MIX
Paper from
responsible sources
FSC® C144853

THE OLD LIBRARY

TITLE: FRANKENSTILTSKIN
AUTHOR: JOSEPH COELHO

DATE	NAME
04/01/85	B. Grimm
30/08/97	M.W.S.

To the child brave enough
to keep reading!!!! – J.C.

For my brothers Fin and Inigo
who love a good spooky story! – F.H.

CONTENTS

The Librarian

Hello, repulsive readers.
I am The Librarian
of fairy tales that have gone bad.

I wasn't always this way.
I used to be a librarian
of lovely books, quaint, sweet,
well-regarded, twee books.
But then I ventured
to the back of the library
and found a forgotten shelf
where the books had gone off
like sour milk.
    Become rotten,
like bin juice.
But in their rot
they revealed the truth within tales,
without any of the gloss
to make them more ... palatable.

As I read these books
I started to change.
The books made me their keeper,
their protector.

I have since found
more festering tales
and my shelf has become
a whole bookcase of fairy tales
that have gone bad!
And as my collection grows ...
I, too, change and become something ... other!!!

You may think you know
the story of *Rapunzel*.
Well, in my library the books
know the true story
and its true title ...

Flu-punzle!

And you may think you know the tale
of *Snow White and the Seven Dwarves*...

Well, that fairy tale should really be called ...
**Snow Fright and her Seven
Hungry Wolves.**

I have one of my favourites
here just for you.
You may have heard
of the story of *Rumpelstiltskin*.
Well, my books have revealed
the true tale.
It's a story thread
of monstrous endings
and a well-stitched beginning.
This is the tale of ...

FRANKENSTILTSKIN.
MUHA ha ha ha ha ha ha...

CHAPTER 1

Wet-Tail

Bryony loved animals,
loved them.
Every kind,
every shape, every size,
from sliming worms
to hopping frogs,
from bellowing unicorns
to yapping dogs,
she loved them all.
Her love was in part
due to her job.
Bryony was a taxidermist.
A stuffer of animal skins
for educational shenanigans.

Today she had been called out
to the outskirts of town
where a farmer had found out
about the body of a very rare bird.

She arrived at the site
as the sun dipped its light
and met the farmer at the tragic sight.

A dodo bird found dead,
dead as a dodo.
A rare and marvellous animal.
The cause of its demise?
A severe case of extinction!

The farmer knew
Bryony's work
from the local museum,
where her displays awed school students,
aided veterinary practitioners

and broadened the minds of the general public.

He knew that this poor creature
would be a valued addition
to the collection.

"A terrible shame to catch Extinction so young,"
said the farmer,
wiping his eyes
with a grimed handkerchief
as he left Bryony to her mournful work.

Bryony snapped on her gloves,
held the bird's heavy body
in her careful hands,
closed her eyes and was ...

transported.

In her mind's eye
Bryony could see the dodo waddling
over the grey rocks
and purple tussocks of its home,
enjoying the views
of the ocean beyond.

She loved these Death-Dreams,
she had them every time
she touched an animal hide.
It was a special gift
that gave her the means to
connect with the animals
she worked on,
to see how life had been
for them.
To see how best
to honour them in death.
Through this gift,
Bryony was able to educate

and inform, and ... stuff!
Bryony took her time
carefully packing
the poor dodo in ice
and solemnly walked back home.

As she threaded her way
through the needle country lanes
on the outskirts
of her sleepy little town,
Bryony heard the bugle call
of the fire-drake dragon hunters.

They were merciless hunters
who she hated,
always wanting to employ her services
for their trophies.
But Bryony and her father always refused,
only ever using their taxidermy skills
on animals that had died natural deaths.
The hunters chased these poor
magical creatures
with their ice-throwing water pistols
to extinguish their flicker,
claiming they were stopping
the spread of fire,
though everyone knew
that fire-drakes
only caused fires
if threatened.

Bryony longed for the return
of Chain-Breaker Jack,
a freedom fighter
for animals everywhere.
No one knew who he was,
but he would appear
wherever animals were in need.
Chain-Breaker Jack had saved
fire-drakes in the past,
with his flowing robes
and impenetrable shield.
But he had not been seen
for a very long time.
So now the hunters,
trappers and furriers
were amassing,
exercising their right
to trap and hunt,
a right set in stone by
The King of all Mythica.

A flash of flame flew past
as a fire-drake
zipped its fiery body
around Bryony.
An ice-cold water jet
followed behind it,
extinguishing its flame.
It crashed into a bush.
The bugle calls got louder
as the hunters clattered
around the corner,
riding their mechanical beasts
of heat and steam.

"Girl!"
yelled a large sweaty man
atop his metallic monstrosity
that looked like a barrel with legs.

"Have you seen a fire-drake around here?"
"No," said Bryony, quickly stepping in front
of the fire-drake's hiding place.
"They're incredibly rare."

"Not rare enough, if you ask us,"
said the sweaty man as he tossed a sweaty flap
of sweaty hair over his sweaty balding pate.

*"You look hot, maybe you should stop
hunting a poor defenceless animal."*

"Ha! Stop! Never!" said the sweaty man
before sounding his bugle and leading
the hunters off on their mechanical terrors.

25

Once they were gone,
Bryony bent down to the bush
and gasped.
She had never seen
a fire-drake up close before,
most people only glimpsed
flashes of flame in the distance.
It was incredibly rare to see one
extinguished and up close.
It was gently smouldering,
its skin was jet black and scaly
and its large green eyes
looked scared.

"It's OK, you're safe now. They've gone,
you can go home."

Something resembling a smile
flickered over the fire-drake's face.
It puffed its cheeks
and tried to ignite its body flames once again,
but it just sputtered
and nothing more than black smoke
poured from its scales.

"You poor thing. They got you with the ice
water. You'll have to come with me until your
flame is back."

Bryony reached out her hand.
The fire-drake sniffed at it,
crawled onto it,
and continued on up her arm,
perching on her shoulder.

*"That's settled then, I think I shall call you
Wet-Tail in honour of how we met."*

Wet-Tail curled around Bryony's neck,
his warm body comforting her
as she continued home
with her load
of poor dead dodo.

CHAPTER 2

The King

Bryony stuffed animal skins
alongside her taxidermist father.
Animals were her first love
and her tenderness towards them
showed in her careful,

respectful work.
Work that had:
educated the people of Mythica
through beautiful museum displays,
helped in the constant fight for the
conservation of habitats,
and comforted those who had lost their pets.

Bryony loved her job,
loved the joy she could bring to people
on their darkest days,
loved the fact that her art
had helped the public
understand the beauty
and the fragility of the natural world.

Her father said she had...

"Fingers like needles."

The fingers of a true taxidermist,
gentle enough
to handle the skin
of a recently dead Prussian Blue.
Careful enough
to ease the feathers from the corpse
of a cockatoo.

Her father was proud...

Perhaps too proud.

Bryony's father had taught her
everything he knew
on the goose-pimpling delight
of taxidermy...

Taxidermy

*Definition: The art and practice of stuffing,
displaying and mounting animal skins for
museum, scientific or private display.*

Just like his mother had taught him
and her grandmother had taught her,
it was a family business as shown on their
business cards...

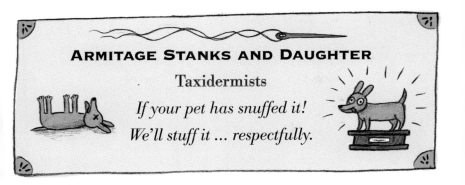

ARMITAGE STANKS AND DAUGHTER

Taxidermists

If your pet has snuffed it!
We'll stuff it ... respectfully.

Bryony was good.
Some said "unnaturally good."
Her father was her biggest fan
and would continually
boast about her uncanny skill...

"You'll never need mourn,
your pet will be reborn.
With a quick cut and a snip,
she'll reanimate it."

In fact, he did more than say as much:
he shouted about it,
created a campaign about it,

33

painted the shop front with the bold
statement.
All to Bryony's dismay.
Bryony was a humble and modest
taxidermist.

Word got around
their sleepy little town
and spread to the other
sleepy little towns of all Mythica
and soon their little shop
was bursting at the seams
with customers.
Through the Death-Dreams
she experienced when touching
the animal hides,
Bryony was able to create
the most natural and lifelike poses:

A tabby cat
  curled up on a mat.

A pug
  asleep on a rug.

A beagle
    looking regal.

A cockatoo
    doing a ... crossword!

The customers were amazed,
and Bryony's father was rich!
Richer than he'd ever been,
able to expand the premises,
to stuff bigger animals
from richer clients
and bigger organizations.
He was able to extend his advertising
to billboards...

ARMITAGE STANKS AND DAUGHTER

Bring back animals from the ever after.

To the sides of buses...

Visit taxidermists
ARMITAGE STANKS AND DAUGHTER
by bus, bring your pets back from Anubis.

Covering the tops of skyscrapers...

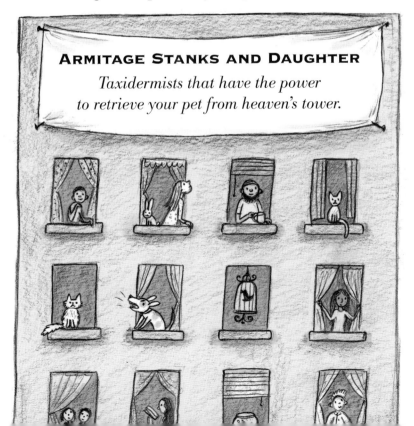

ARMITAGE STANKS AND DAUGHTER
*Taxidermists that have the power
to retrieve your pet from heaven's tower.*

It was on a hot summer's day
that Armitage Stanks and Daughter
got their grandest customer yet.

A King,
not just any King
but The King of all Mythica
and its surrounding sleepy hamlets.

Little had been seen
of The King since the illness and death
of his only son – Prince Tiberius.

King Theocritus was younger
than Bryony would have imagined.
A slim dark-skinned man
with startling hazel eyes,
dressed in a ceremonial suit of armour
of copper, bronze and gold.
He viewed the many specimens

that adorned
Armitage Stanks and Daughter's little shop,
tutting and shaking his head like one in a strop.

"Is this your best work?"

he asked Bryony's father,
as Bryony peered on from the back studio,
her hands delicately setting
the scene for a poor dead jackrabbit
with Wet-Tail gently simmering on her shoulder.

Armitage Stanks floundered.
Unused to anything less than high praise,
he was eager to impress...

"This is MY best work, your majesty,
but nothing comes close
to the work of my daughter,
a genius, a prodigy, a miracle..."

And that's when all the
advertising slogans he'd been dreaming up
came gushing forth...

"She can breathe new life into your dead pets,
make it as if they never went to the vets.

Take a dead parakeet,
and give it back it's tweet.

Recover a mole
from that six-foot-deep hole.

For her fingers are long,
her fingers are quick.
They're magical fingers,
that stitch, stitch, stitch!

With her skills
in taxidermy,
she can deliver faster than Hermes
every dear pet you may have lost.

She can restore your flattened cat,
have him purring on the mat.

No doubt a king has a menagerie,
of animal skins from every family.
My daughter can return life
to the whole wonderful lot!"

The King's interest piqued.

"You claim your daughter's skills are ...
extra-ordinary?"

"The best in the land."

"And she can bring life back to the dead?"

"Why yes
*   (in a manner of speaking).*
Absolutely
*   (small print allowing).*
Without a doubt, I guarantee it, my daughter is
a miracle worker."

That's when The King clapped his hands thrice...

Clap.

Clap.

Clap.

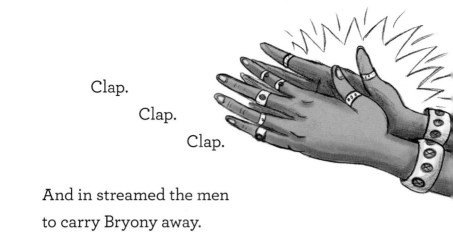

And in streamed the men
to carry Bryony away.

CHAPTER 3

The Labyrinth Palace

Bryony was bundled
into one of The King's many carriages
to a part of Mythica she'd never been to
before –
The Labyrinth of Palaces.
The horses galloped
through The Scab Gate,
the huge rusted-iron entrance
to The Labyrinth of Palaces.
From her window
Bryony was shocked at how different
this private city was compared to her little
hamlet.

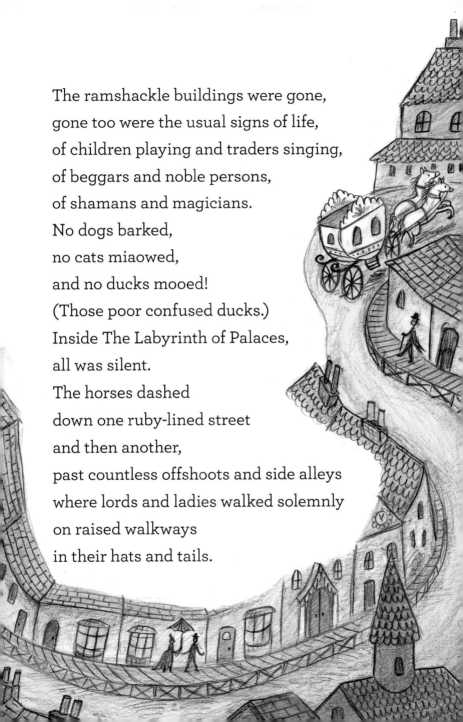

The ramshackle buildings were gone,
gone too were the usual signs of life,
of children playing and traders singing,
of beggars and noble persons,
of shamans and magicians.
No dogs barked,
no cats miaowed,
and no ducks mooed!
(Those poor confused ducks.)
Inside The Labyrinth of Palaces,
all was silent.
The horses dashed
down one ruby-lined street
and then another,
past countless offshoots and side alleys
where lords and ladies walked solemnly
on raised walkways
in their hats and tails.

"This is The Labyrinth of Palaces, girl,
built over millennia by countless kings and
queens, each adding to this mad private
city we call home."

Her Feather-Masked Guard revelled in being
her unofficial guide.
He pointed to the jagged buildings as they
passed...

"These palaces are the oldest,
built in the reign of our first queen,
Queen Alina the Thirsty
in the time before times.
Most are empty now, of course."

The horses started to climb,
Bryony was flung back into her seat.
The ruby-lined streets gave way to
pink-cobblestone boulevards of shops.

One shop they passed
had its windows boarded up,
'Out of Business' signs painted over its walls.

"That WAS the royal taxidermist,"

said her guard,
fixing her with a threatening stare.

The carriage continued on.
Bryony could swear they went up some streets
twice or even thrice
in opposite directions.

"Are we lost?"
she asked.

"Lost!" guffawed the guard.
"Girl, we are ALL lost in The Labyrinth
of Palaces."
The road ended at a rock face
of bone-white marble
and the carriage stopped.
She craned her neck skywards,
through the carriage's windows.
It was a mountain of marble with green outcrops
of vegetation dotted over its surface.
At its peak was a palace,
carved out of the mountain's summit.

A worry-of-staff unharnessed the horses
and replaced them with huge goats,
the largest goats Bryony had ever seen,
their eyes a liquid gold,
their horns like tree crowns.

Her guard tied himself into the carriage seat
with thick ropes.
"You better do likewise if you
don't want to get a bruising."

She sat down and did as the guard
commanded. And as she did so,
she heard The King's carriage leave.
But where to? she wondered.
They were at a dead end.
Before she could ponder anymore,
the new giant goat mounts of her carriage
attacked what was left of the road at speed,
and with loud, thunderous bleats
started to climb the rock face,
dragging the carriages behind them.
Bryony was flabbergasted

                        and then terrified
as the guard started to load his blunderbuss.

"Don't shoot!" yelped Bryony.
"This isn't for you," he laughed as
he aimed his blunderbuss upwards.
"I have ta blast the cacti."

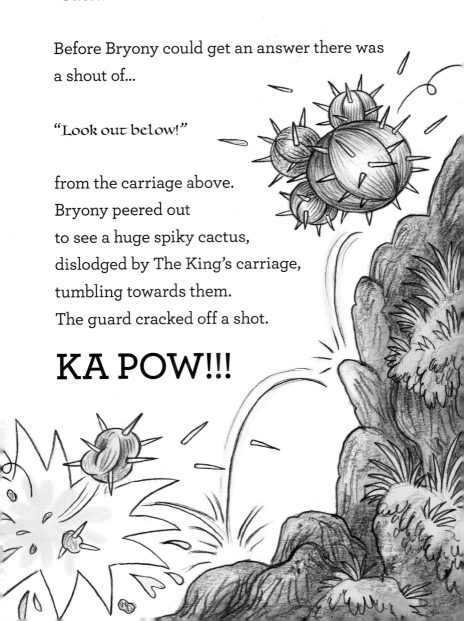

"*Cacti?*"

Before Bryony could get an answer there was
a shout of...

"Look out below!"

from the carriage above.
Bryony peered out
to see a huge spiky cactus,
dislodged by The King's carriage,
tumbling towards them.
The guard cracked off a shot.

KA POW!!!

"Got it!" he laughed.

Cacti spines the size of spears rained past them,
a few striking the carriage head-on
and poking through into the interior.

"*That was close!*" breathed Bryony,
her fear now tinged with awe.

"For you maybe," came the guard's grizzled reply.
A cacti spine had jabbed him in his shoulder!
Bryony sprang into action,
tearing material from the guard's sleeve
and stuffing it around the wound. "Leave me!
Shoot or we'll be smashed to cacti pulp."

Bryony was confused,
but then heard another call of...

"Look out below."

Realization hit.

Bryony took up the blunderbuss,
and leaned out of the window.
She could see a huge cactus
tumbling straight for them.

"SHOOT, GIRL!"

There was no time to panic – Bryony had to shoot!
She took three quick breaths,
aimed and fired three quick shots...

BLAST!

BANG!

BOOM!

The boulder-sized cacti
exploded into a rain of pulp.

Bryony was relieved
when the carriages reached the summit
and they were back on level ground.
The view from the marble mountaintop
was magnificent; she could see the whole
of Mythica.
Their goats trotted up to the palace's entrance.
It was beautiful.
Four huge spiralled towers defined its corners
with windows that looked
like they could blink.
The central spire was
squat and shaped like a human skull.
"You better wait here,"
huffed her guard as he struggled from
the carriage
with his cactus spine injury.

The sweat pooled in Bryony's hands.

She wasn't expecting the bag that came
swooping down over her head,
blindfolding her to the world as she was
pushed into
The King's palace.

CHAPTER 4

Skin of a Wolf

Bryony's introduction to the palace
was one of sensations.
She was pulled and dragged
this way and that,
impossibly down,
unbelievably up,
through corridors and passageways
as topsy-turvy
as the streets taken by the carriages.
There were times when she was made to
crawl on her hands and knees
through things wet and warm.
Her only comfort was Wet-Tail's warmth,
as he lay hidden inside her taxidermist's apron.

When the sack
was finally peeled
from her head,
Bryony found herself in a large bedroom
of sumptuous design.
It was far grander than any
she had been in before,
the redwood floors
polished to a mirror shine,
a bed as big
as her room at home ...
bigger!

But the main attraction
was a huge metal table that sat
between the fireplace
with its sputtering fire,
and a wide ebony grandfather clock
that quietly tocked.

63

On the table were all the implements
Bryony used for her taxidermy work:
scalpels and scissors,
wire and wool,
clay and hay,
pins for skins,
fixing solutions and alcohol dilutions,
and a hairdryer!

"Rest now," said her guard
who was slightly less gruff now
and slightly more ruffled
as he huffled
with the pain of his cactus spine wound.
"You will have your instructions soon enough."
As he closed the door
he tapped his bandages with a wince and said...
"Thank you, girl, that was brave
and too kind for an old gruffian like me
and sorry about the blindfold –
The King trusts no one,"
before locking it behind him.
And that's when the smell hit her.
A familiar lingering scent,
a smell that hid beneath the aroma of
the many scented candles
that were blazing in the room,
a smell that crept when you weren't looking.

She followed her nose,
snuffing out the
scented candles as she went,
intensifying the sickly scent.

Her nose led her to a door
she hadn't seen before.
A round wooden door.
She turned the black ebony handle
and found it locked.

She levelled her eye to the keyhole,
the rancid smell was stronger there.
In the room beyond, all she could make out was
a huge dark shape,
silhouetted in the low light
of that mysterious place.
The floor by this door was deeply scratched.
The scratches led
to the unusually wide grandfather clock.
How strange! she thought.
The smell was getting bad.
Bryony snatched up
the matches from a small bedside table
and tried to relight the candles.
But the matches were old and wouldn't take.

Wet-Tail peeped out from under her apron,
ran down her arm and hiccupped a small flame.
It was all he could manage,
his fiery body flame had still not returned.
But at least he could do this.
As Bryony watched the candles burn
she wondered how long The King
would keep her here,
wondered what task
he could possibly have for her,
wondered if she would ever
see her loving father again.

The door to her room was flung open
and in walked the tallest,
thinnest man Bryony had ever seen.
He looked as if he had been strung out,
stretched out,

       spaghettified.

"Good day to you, Bryony,
I am Yeltsin Thorogood
The Tongue of The King –
Order-Giver,
Praise-Bestower
and Insult-Hurler.
The King was mightily impressed
by your father's claims of your ability
in taxidermy.
He has asked me
to request of you
that you do
what it is you do."

"He wants me to stuff an animal for him?"

"Stuff ... no,
your father's claims
went beyond the mere stuffing.
If it was merely a stuffing The King wanted,

the royal taxidermist
would still be in with a job
and a home
and a reputation
and all of his socks.
No, Bryony, he wants you
to work your magic
to ... how did your father put it..."

Yeltsin Thorogood angled his long fingers
into one of his deep pockets
and teased out one of her father's flyers...

ARMITAGE STANKS AND DAUGHTER

Bring yer pets back from the ever after.

"*The King requires you to use this skill
to bring back something precious to him.*"

And with that Yeltsin Thorogood
pointed his long feet
towards the round door
at the corner of the room,
strode over there in two neat lengths,
and from a long chain
hanging around his narrow waist,
he drew forth a thin key.

"Stand back,"

he said as he poked his long nose
down the collar of his skinny shirt,
unlocked the round door and slid inside,
allowing Bryony not so much as a peek
at what lay beyond.

Within moments Yeltsin was sliding back
around the door,
slamming it shut
and locking it tight.
In his slender hand
he held the skin of a wolf.
It was black and grey,
the pelt of a once beautiful animal.

"You want me to stuff this wolf?"

*"No! Certainly not! The King
requires you to bring this wolf
back to LIFE!"*

"Back to LIFE... But I'm not a miracle worker,
I'm a taxidermist,
an animal stuffer,
an artist,
a preserver and rejoicer of life
that once was."

Yeltsin Thorogood turned on her,
something new,
something sad,
dewing in his long-eyelashed eyes.

"We must all do what we can
for The King and his needs.
Your father has made ambitious claims
and I am sure your father is not a liar?"

"Well... No...
He likes to be creative with language.
But my father is no liar..."

"Well, then ... if your father is no liar
there should be no problem..."

"But!"

"You have until 3pm tomorrow."

And with that Yeltsin Thorogood
towered out of the room,
locking Bryony,
her tears
and the wolf skin
within.

CHAPTER 5

A Strange Visitor

Bryony was furious.

She wept fuming tears, angry at her father
for exaggerating her skill.

She wept boiling tears, angry at The King
for wanting the impossible.

She wept and raged around
the stinking room,
throwing the cushions off the bed,
banging on the door and walls.

Wet-Tail watched,
eyes wide with worry,
cold ash puffing nervously from his scales.

When her anger and tears were spent
she peered down at the wolf skin
on the metal table.
It was beautiful.
She ran her fingers through its thick,
silky fur, closed her eyes,
and was ...

Bryony was in a forest ...
a dark forest,
where crying could be heard.
Bryony walked between the dark trees
as the moonlight streamed down,
following the crying,
and she came upon
the wolf. Now she could see
from the way it mewled
that even though it was big,
it was still just a puppy,
a big, orphaned puppy.
Bryony cried out in alarm,
but no sound issued from her lips.
She ran to the pup,
desperate to hold it to her,
to comfort it.
But as she reached for it
her hands passed through it.

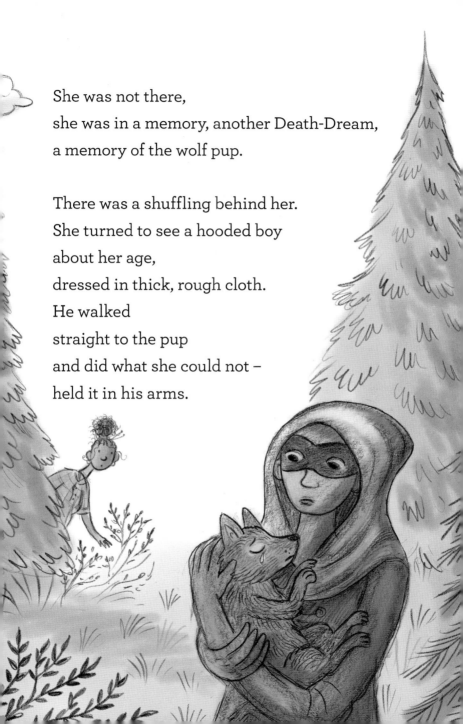

She was not there,
she was in a memory, another Death-Dream,
a memory of the wolf pup.

There was a shuffling behind her.
She turned to see a hooded boy
about her age,
dressed in thick, rough cloth.
He walked
straight to the pup
and did what she could not –
held it in his arms.

"Hello, big pup,
have those damn trappers taken your mother?"
he hissed.
"You're coming with me, little one,
to my secret menagerie
for all injured and lost animals,
where you will have all the time and space
you need to grow and get strong.
You will return to these woods, I promise you.
These woods will be safe once again
or my name isn't Chain-Breaker Jack."

Bryony opened her eyes
and was back in the bedroom,
the wolf pup's pelt laid out in front of her.
She had seen Chain-Breaker Jack,
famed rescuer of animals.
He had saved this wolf pup,
but how had it ended up here
in the palace?

She didn't have time to think on it.
She had to make a start on stuffing the wolf.
Now she had seen it in her Death-Dream
it would be easier.

Bryony snapped on her rubber gloves.
She could feel the old thrill
of her taxidermy skill
returning to her.
Feel her artist's eye appraising the deceased,
deciding how best to honour the beast.
But ... it was pointless.
The King expected her
to bring the wolf back to life!
To do the impossible.
She could feel the tears of frustration
bubbling up again
when, to her hair-raising shock,
she heard a laugh...

A sinister, chittering laugh...

Wet-Tail ran to her
and cowered on her shoulder.
From the locked round door
in the corner of the room
came a creaking
and a squeaking
as the wood started to strain and rumble.
A smaller door appeared within the larger one,
no taller than her knees,
and it was opening,
spilling a waft of that sickly scent.
The fingers that slid around the door
were long, grimy and thin,
the nails dirty.
The feet that poked around the door
were broad and hairy,
the nails clawed.

The face that wrapped around the door
was small and cunning,
the smile mischievous.

Wet-Tail sputtered nervously at the creature
that slunk around that small door.
A child-sized creature,

but by the wrinkles in his face
he was old, ancient.
His skin was dirty and scarred,
the crosshatching of long-healed stitches
zigzagged his face
and framed
his mismatched eyes.
He looked like a stitched combination
of many different things.
One of his ears was long, pointed and red
like that of a fox,
his snout was part dog, part man.
His skin was bald in patches, hairy in others
and he was dressed in a
patchwork of leathers.
Bryony got ready to run and scream.
The creature's beady eyes drank her in.
He flicked
out his long fingers
and Bryony was frozen to the spot.

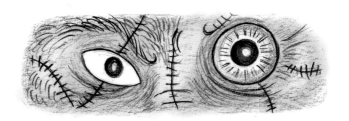

"There is nowhere to run, my pet,
When I've come to set you free.
I wouldn't shout and scream,
At a magical creature such as me.

I may be small and hairy,
And my stature somewhat wanting.
I may be strange and scary.
But your task is far more daunting.

The King requires the impossible,
From a mere girl with limited skill.
The King demands new life,
From a wolf that is quite still.

Sure, you can stuff a parrot,
And display an orchestra of mice.
Sure, you can preserve a coyote,
And an elephant, for the right price.

But the spark of life escapes you,
You're yet to learn that power.
The ability to mock death,
Is not a subject for an innocent flower.

But never fear, my pet,
For I have arrived.
You can leave this task to me,
I'll bring this wolf back from the other side."

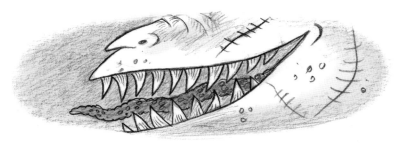

He strode over to the large metal table
where the wolf skin lay.

"You haven't even begun,"
he snapped, releasing Bryony from his spell.

"Of course not!" she gasped.
"It's an impossible task."

"Everything is impossible before you start,"
he sneered.

"But I can't make it live..."

"Live! Leave the living to me, pet,
just you worry
about stuffing the wolfdog
and don't rush the job!
Make it a stuffed dog
worthy of your slog."

A thousand questions ran through
Bryony's mind.
But she feared The King's wrath
and wanted to get home to her father.
So, Bryony sat at the large metal table,
picked up her needle and thread ...

and began.

CHAPTER 6

Live

Bryony worked through the night
and late into the following day.
The strange little creature hopping and
dancing around her, telling her to...

"Hurry up,
Don't give up.
Snip and sew with care."

It was by far her best work.
She had posed the wolf pup mid-step,
his mouth slightly open, slightly smiling.
She had used black opals for the eyes
and they danced with an inner sparkle.

She had wished it was a specimen
going to the museum where she and her father
sent most of their work to be studied by academics
and wowed at by visitors.

"The work is good," growled the little creature.

A chime rang out in the room, the ebony
grandfather clock had started its strike for 3 o'clock.

Bryony could hear footsteps approaching.
Her deadline was up,
and the wolf was still ... still!
What would become of her?

Bryony started to panic,
started to sweat and pace...

"He'll lock me up, imprison me!
Take all my socks!"

That's when the little creature
leapt onto the big table,
circling his hands above his head
and muttering in a language
that was thick and strange.
A dark mist spooled out of his palms
and gathered into a ball of swaying,
undulating energy.

"Trust in me, my pet,
I can make the wolf live.
The only thing that matters,
is how much you want to give."

The footsteps were getting louder.
Bryony rooted her hands into the pockets
of her taxidermist's trousers and apron,
searching for something
to give the little creature.
Nothing.

She checked her neck for her necklace.
No! She could not give that.
She rang her fingers through her curls
and an idea hit.

She swiped up the scissors
and cut a lock from her hair
and thrust it at the creature.

"A token of my thanks,
a lock of my hair.
Some say it is as deep
and radiant as the night."

The creature smiled
through rotten teeth.
He nodded his approval
and with a loud bang
sent the spiralling ball of black mist
down into the body of the wolf.
The room went dark,
thunder sounded
though none of the windows were open.
The creature's eyes glowed
with a dark energy
as he threw his
head back
and shouted...

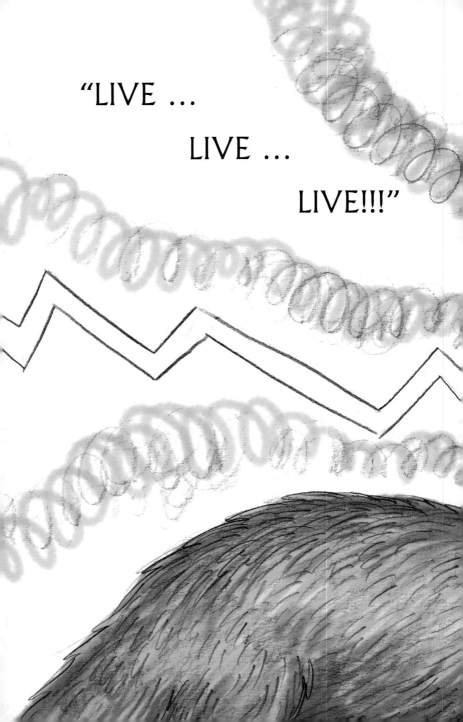

Sparks of electricity
flickered over the wolf's body
and then it
writhed and wreathed
and breathed!
Slowly at first,
coughing up a cloud of hay dust.
It started to move,
testing the stiff wires that
Bryony had threaded through its limbs,
warming them up until ...

it trotted

then ran

then raced

around the room,
barking its strange bark
and leaping as it went.
Wet-Tail leapt
onto the central chandelier with fright.

105

The door swung open and
in came The King, followed by
The Feather-Masked Guard
and Yeltsin Thorogood,
their faces
a muddlement of astonishment.
The strange little creature
and Bryony's lock of obsidian hair ...

were gone.

CHAPTER 7

Unbearable

That night
was a night of celebration.
The King was jubilant.
Bryony was made his guest
in the great osseous,

bonafide –

bone-ified! – dinner hall,
with its bone-like walls and floor.

108

She was presented with the greatest feast
she had ever seen.
There were roasted spiders
and fried guinea pigs,
bubbling stews and
quivering breads.

Wet-Tail climbed down from
Bryony's shoulder and sniffed at
the foodstuffs, a curl of smoke
snaking out from under his black scales.

"It's OK, Wet-Tail, we don't have to eat it,"
she murmured to him.

"I will not eat meat
or anything made from an animal,"
Bryony declared defiantly to The King
as the dishes were laid on.
The King eyed her
with a look of bending steel.

"Bring the girl something she can eat.
Something from the prince's old menu."
The chef, a portly man
wearing the tallest chef's hat that
Bryony had ever seen,

appeared at her side
with a menu.

"Perhaps you wish
to pick a dish
from this."

The menu was faded.
At the top it said:

The Prince's Royal Vegan Menu.

There were starters of beetroot sautéed in
orange juice,
parsnip crisps with cashew cheese dip,
mains of pulse loaves
with cauliflower steaks.
Bryony's mouth was watering.

Bryony and Wet-Tail filled their stomachs
as The King looked on
and the wolf pup
ran around and barked and leapt.

It ran to The Feather-Masked Guard,
who laughed deeply
as he stroked the wolf's long fur,
even though his injury clearly still pained him
with each guffaw.

It ran to Yeltsin Thorogood,
who smiled down at the excitable pup
and tenderly stroked each ear
with his long fingers.

The King called the wolf pup
over to him with a glint in his eye.

"Here now!"
The wolf's tail immediately stopped wagging,
its ears drooped down.

It slowly plodded over to The King
who roughly stroked its fur
(in the wrong direction)
and grabbed its maw,
inspecting it as one would
a piece of over-ripe fruit.
The wolf pined softly,
and a dent formed in The King's eyes.

"The work is good.
Wouldn't you say so, Thorogood?"
asked The King.
Thorogood nodded and smiled,
his narrow eyes
constantly flicking over to Bryony.

*"The girl has done wonders, my King,
perhaps we should send her home?"*

"Wonders indeed,"
clanged The King, before erupting
into a slow soupy laugh.

*"If my lord is happy with my work,
then may I humbly ask that I be returned home
to my father, I know he misses me."*

That's when the mood changed,
when the last chatter of laughter
echoed throughout the osseous hall
and crumbled.
The King wiped his mouth,
the iron pouring back into his eyes.

"You will leave when your work is done."

With one final cutting look,
The King spun around
and left the osseous hall,
his heels tapping a dirge.

Once he was gone,
Yeltsin Thorogood
urged Bryony out of the hall
and back to her room, her prison.

"What did I say?"
she asked.

"The King has more work for you yet,"

Yeltsin replied as he removed the long key
from the long chain
that snaked his narrow waist
and opened the round door
in the bedroom,
from whence the stench crept.

He slid inside, closing the door behind him.
Moments later she heard him
huffing from the other side
of the round door,
and then struggling and clambering at its handle.
The door yawned open
as Yeltsin shuffled through it, this time
with the skin of a gigantic ...

polar bear!

CHAPTER 8

Jack's Army

Bryony was furious.
Here she was again,
locked in the room,
this time with the skin
of a gigantic polar bear,
expected to do the impossible.

She thumped the walls,
kicked the grandfather clock,

threw the feathers out of her pillows,
and stopped,
the hairs lifted on the back of her neck.
She heard the creaking
of the small hidden door
as, once again,
the bent little creature
with the hairy feet
and patchwork skin
oozed into the room.
But something about him was different.

His hair was as black and as luscious as Bryony's.
Wet-Tail flared into flame with fright,
but he couldn't hold the flame for long.
He smouldered sheepishly
in the corner of the room,
eyeing the little creature
who burst into song...

"Oh dear, my pet,
What a pickle you're in,
The King has another impossible task.

He wants you to animate
this Arctic furry weight,
And throw off its heavy death-mask.

You bawl and scream,
And throw a fit,
But, my pet, time is ticking.

If you don't get
this rug to move,
Your life won't be worth living.

But never fear,
My feisty dear,
Your friend will not leave you wanting.

I will help you
with this burden,
I'll get this rotter walking.

But in return,
If you will?
A little favour for my chore.

A gift from you,
Of something new,
A little thing for me to adore."

Bryony hunted in her pockets,
but there was nothing she could give.
She bit her lip as she thought,
and an idea struck.
She had no choice.
She opened the locket
that hung round her neck
and took from it her last milk tooth,
the last one to fall out
after her mother had left,
the one she denied the tooth fairies,
despite how much they begged for it.

It was a small, brilliantly white tooth.
She handed it to the little creature and said...

"I am told my smile is pearl white."

The horrid little thing nodded,
and, with each nod,
Bryony noticed the foul stench
that wafted up from his mouth.

"Work now and make your work good."

Bryony ran her fingers
through the bear's hair,
closed her eyes
and was ...

In her Death-Dream, Bryony could see
the giant polar bear
steeped in sadness
in a cage on a tiny island of ice
floating on a mirror sea.
Impossibly large boats
roared through the water
with terrifying
signs on their sides...

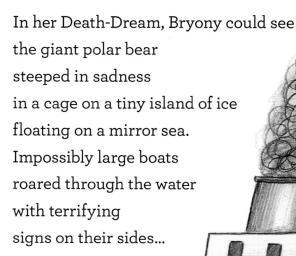

**_Bear trappers
by royal appointment_**

The filthy men
on the large boats
laughed and sang
as they continued
their foul work.

"We work all day
and we sail all day
all over the briny sea.
We sharpen our sticks
and we prod quick, quick, quick,
these giant bear beasties.

We burn our coal
and heat the seas
as we travel far and wide.
We melt the ice
and blacken the sky
on our search for the softest hides."

Bryony watched
as the men cackled and sang.
That was until
another boat arrived.
A huge boat
blown on the wind
with sails like dragon wings
and golden cannons lining its sides.

"Give up this poor bear,
or prepare to meet the wrath
of Chain-Breaker Jack."

Bryony was back in her body,
amazed at what the polar bear's hide
had revealed to her.
She still remembered the fear
she saw in the bear's eyes,
the gentleness and terror,
and its relief at being saved
by Chain-Breaker Jack.
She wanted to bring the bear back,
wanted to give him another chance
at life.

Bryony went to work
throughout the night
cleaning the gigantic polar bear skin,
washing it,
scrubbing it until it shone,
stuffing it with hay and clay,
moulding a body for it,
placing black garnets in its eyes
and sewing it all tightly back together.
It was hard, laborious work
requiring both skill and strength
as she pulled and tugged
the massive skin
over the bear-shaped framework
she had created.

Bryony worked
right up until the clock
started to chime
for her deadline –
3 o'clock on the dot
whether she liked it or not.
Footsteps could be heard
coming down the corridor,
Yeltsin and The King coming to check
on her progress.
As promised,
the foul little creature
filled his hands
with the darkest smoke,
and smote
the polar bear
with a terrible sorcery.
Suddenly, the bear lifted its huge mass,
bent its shaggy head ...

and roared a roar
that could frighten stone.

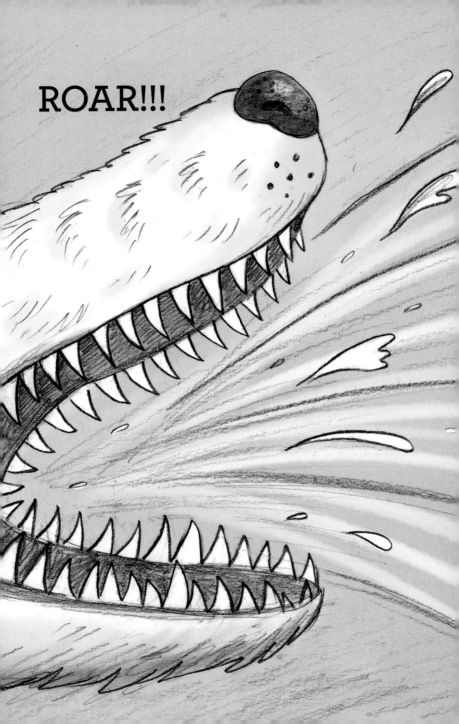

CHAPTER 9

To Question a King

The King was ecstatic
and once again Bryony was made
his guest of honour.
This time the chefs were prepared for
her vegan diet. There were:
glazed pineapple rings,
seaweed crisps,
flower petal lasagnas,
achocha salads
and lemony oca bites.

She was famished from her work
stuffing the giant polar bear,
but too angry to eat.
Her anger bubbled.
Wet-Tail could sense it,
and little smoking embers wafted up from under
his scales.
Bryony stood up suddenly from the bone-white table
and marched down the osseous hall
until she was face to face with The King.

"I'd sit down, girl, if I were you,"

came the gentle but firm warning
from The Feather-Masked Guard.
"It's OK. Let her speak,"
said The King
as he scooped the seeds
from a pomegranate.

"You're a monster!"
A gasp echoed around the hall
from the smattering of staff.

"Am I?" chimed The King, coolly.

"Yes, you are, you care nothing for the people
of your so-called kingdom and even less for
the animals.
You allow them to be hunted, trapped
and caged."

There was silence in
the hall as a small careful smile
ratcheted into place on The King's face,
that quickly became a mechanical guffaw.

"You know nothing, girl,
of me, or my kingdom,
or the sacrifices I have made.
The land, the sea, the meadows,
the forests, the fields
and all the animals within them
are mine. MINE. To do with as I please."

Bryony was returned to her seat
by the Feather-Masked Guard.
She wanted revenge.
But I am useless if I am weak,
I must build my strength,
she thought as the food was piled up.
The atmosphere in the hall eased.
So she ate
and chewed
and swallowed
and gulped her food down.
Not tasting any of it.
Wet-Tail crouched by her plate
sampling everything before she did
like a little royal taster.

The King
clapped and bellowed
a hollow laugh
as the bear Bryony had stuffed
was brought out,
and made to dance
to the music of a piper
who nervously piped a sad tune.

Bryony started to grind her teeth
and set her resolve on revenge.

CHAPTER 10

Jailbreak

It was dark.
Bryony awoke
to the sound of The Feather-Masked Guard
pacing her room.
He was the definition of agitation.

"I can't defy The King.
    But The King has gone too far.
But I am a dutiful guard.
    But where will this madness end?"

144

"What's wrong?" said Bryony, sitting bolt
upright in bed,
Wet-Tail growling by her side.

"I'm sorry, girl.
You have to leave, before it's too late.
The King has gone mad.
Ever since you brought
the prince's animals back to life,
The King has had some unnatural ideas!
He's going to ask you to bring back something
that should not be brought back."

The guard turned to the round door
and ripped the wallpaper that surrounded it
revealing a sign...

Tiberius' Menagerie for Sick and Abandoned Animals

"Young Tiberius loved animals,
travelled the world saving them.
But after the sickness took him,
The King fell into a deep melancholy.
He shut up the young prince's bedroom,
this room...

"This round door was hidden behind his
grandfather clock.
None of us knew the menagerie was here.
Not until a maid noticed the smell."

Bryony looked at the deep scratches on the floor,
the ones she had noticed
when she first arrived.

The guard
unlocked the round door.
That subtle, putrid, damp smell
dripped into the bedroom.

"When The King realized that he had
locked up
not just the prince's bedroom but also his
secret menagerie
and all the animals within it,
he felt terrible.
He made me wallpaper over the sign,
he didn't want to be reminded of this..."

Bryony followed the guard
through the round door.
He pulled a long chain
and the lights buzzed on revealing ...

the biggest mound of animal skins
Bryony had ever seen:

Giant zebras,
frost-coloured unicorn pelts,
red gorilla furs,
gigantic spider husks,
oversized mouse skins,
alligator hides,
chameleon skins,
yeti rugs,
phoenix feathers,
humungous boar leathers,
massive angel fish scales.

"This was the young prince's
menagerie, all the animals he had saved
and was bringing back to health,"

said the guard.

"Because you see,
the prince had a secret identity,
he was in fact Chain-Breaker Jack."

Bryony gasped as she took in
what the guard was saying.
The prince was Chain-Breaker Jack,
the one she had seen in her Death-Dreams.
It all made sense now,
that's why the animal hides were here,
in the palace.

In the gloom she could make out
the remnants of incredible
enclosures,
paddocks and pens,
tanks and perches.
These animals would have wanted
for nothing.
The menagerie was vast,
and like everything in The Labyrinth of
Palaces, felt never-ending.

As she followed the guard through the
menagerie
she became aware of grass beneath her feet
and of the ceiling
giving way to the night sky.

The menagerie opened out onto a vast open plain on a craggy cliff edge.

"The prince created a paradise
for all the animals he rescued.
A place where they could recover
without anyone disturbing them.
Especially not The King.
The King doesn't care much for animals.
So, the prince hid this from him.
Hid from him the fact that he was
Chain-Breaker Jack."

Bryony peered around the space,
searching for the strange little creature
who had visited her
these last two nights.
Surely he must live out here, somewhere,
wherever **here** was?

"We have to get you out of here, Bryony,
The King is going to ask
the terrible task of you."

The guard walked Bryony
back to the massive mound
of animal skins.
Hidden behind them,
inset into a wall
of the palace,
was a glass casket.
Inside it lay
the body of
Prince Tiberius,
The King's dead son.

"When we discovered this place
The King decided to keep the prince's body here
like a memorial, I guess,
like a tomb.
Somewhere to keep the prince
until he found a way
to bring him back."

A thousand thoughts
came crashing through
Bryony's head all at once...

I have to get out!

He can't want me to bring back his son!

I wonder what it's like to stuff a prince?

This king has issues!

Where does that weird little creature live?

How do I get out?

I wonder how hard it would be to stuff a human?

I should really get out of here!

He's a handsome prince, I could make a cracking display of him...

No ... I must get out!

And that was when The King and Yeltsin
appeared at the round door
of the prince's menagerie.
The King peered from the guard
to Bryony and back again,
his steel eyes only momentarily
flicking over the glass casket
containing the prince,
his son.

"Does the girl know what she must do?"

"Erm ... yes ... she does, my King,"
came the guard's improvised reply.

"Good. Then we must leave her,
to bring my son
back from the ...

dead!!!."

The King clinked out of the room
with Yeltsin Thorogood hot on his heels.

"I'm so sorry. I thought I'd have more time to
get you out,"
whispered the guard.

"But if I do this, I'll get to go home,
he'll send me back to my father?"

"If your time here
has taught you anything, girl,
it should be this...
The King finds it very hard to let things go."

The guard wheeled in her big metal table
with all its implements,
and with a final apology
locked her inside the menagerie.

As Bryony walked around the mound of skins
she was struck by a profound sadness
as the pointlessness of their deaths sank in.
They were animals,
wild animals that had been saved
by the prince as Chain-Breaker Jack.
But once the prince died
they were left, forgotten, lost.
Locked up, abandoned, trapped in a room
that opened out onto a cliff edge
with no means to escape.
With no one to feed them,
they had starved.

She went over to the glass casket
containing the prince's body.
He looked like he was just sleeping.
He would have loved these animals,
he would have been furious to know that
they had met such a tragic end.

But if The King didn't run such a cruel
kingdom,
these animals would never have needed
saving
in the first place.

I'll make The King pay, she thought.
But how?
She ran her hands
over the multitude of pelts,
skins, furs and feathers
that made up the pile
and closed her eyes,
and was ...

transported.

CHAPTER 11

A Memory of a Prince

Bryony found herself
in the menagerie,
but it was back when
all the animals were alive,
the orangutans clambering
up the trees that grew
where the menagerie opened out to the
cliff-edged glade.

There were huge tortoises nibbling thick
green leaves in a muddy swamp,

rabbits with hazel eyes
carolling around a huge pen,
one with a bandaged missing ear,
another with wheels
where his hind legs should be.

Bryony was amazed at the scope of the prince's
secret animal rescue project.
In one vast tank she saw a long flash of
glittering tail from the water's murky depths.

Then she heard the voices.

"I need your power to help me
save the birds."

"Never fear, my little prince,
your friend is here to serve.
I can save those birds
from the trappers they face,
if you only have the nerve
to give to me
a little thing,
a little portion of your wealth.
It is not your coins
or gold I want,
I merely require your health."

Bryony edged around a tank
of greater horned terrapins,
and there she saw
the prince, alive,
and speaking with ...

the creature!

The creature looked
even more haggard than when she had first
seen him,
leaning on a stick to support his weight,
coughing constantly into a leather
handkerchief.

"What a bizarre request.
To give you my health
would be quite impossible."

"Leave possibilities to me,
my prince. If you want the birds saved,
that is my price."

"Then you have it."

"Good. I will collect
when your health is at its most hearty.
But should you want to bargain,
we can play a little game.
You can keep your ruddy health,
if you can only guess my name."

Bryony's Death-Dream shifted
to a new vision. Time had passed.
She was in the prince's bedroom.
The prince was pacing the room,
a newspaper in his hand
with a headline that read...

☀ KINGDOM NEWS ☀

BIRD TRAPPERS WHISKED OFF BY MYSTERIOUS TORNADO. THE KINGDOM IS PERPLEXED.

The little creature appeared
in a billow of black smoke.

"I have come to collect, my prince,
the fee agreed."

"I wish to keep my health and to guess
your name."

"Very well, my prince,
a game, we two, will play.
There is power in a name.
If you can guess mine,
you won't have to pay."

Bryony watched as the prince guessed
and with each attempt he became weaker,
first sitting on his bed when he suggested
Archibald.

Then lying upon it
when he tried
Gundruk.

Then coughing and wheezing
when his final guess of
Luktal

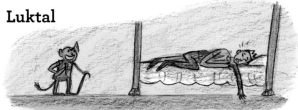

proved to be wrong.

Bryony watched as the prince fell into sickness,
watched the creature
straighten up,
watched his limp disappear,
watched his eyes brighten
and health blossom in his patchwork skin.

Bryony snapped out
of her Death-Dream.
She was alone
with the glass casket
containing the prince
and the mound of skins behind her.
She knew what she had to do.
There was no other way,
it was her only option for freedom.

She gathered up the wires,
clay, hay,
needles and threads
from the large silver table
and set to work.

She worked in a frenzy,
tears becoming a river down her face.
She had to do the unthinkable,
the impossible.
She started sewing
and moulding and stuffing and ...

CREATING!

When the last stitch was in place,
she was startled out of her frenzy
by the slow clap
of the strange little creature.

"You have done well, my pet,"

smiled the creature,
and Bryony noticed
how much like pearls his little teeth now were,
how gorgeous his black hair was,
and exactly like her own.

She looked at her work.
It was by far her best work ever.
But it scared her.

"What will you give me this time
for bringing your creation to life?"
drawled the little thing.

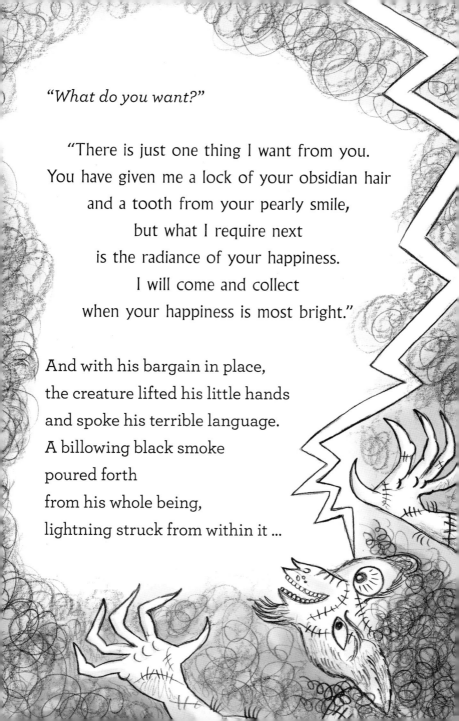

"*What do you want?*"

"There is just one thing I want from you.
You have given me a lock of your obsidian hair
and a tooth from your pearly smile,
but what I require next
is the radiance of your happiness.
I will come and collect
when your happiness is most bright."

And with his bargain in place,
the creature lifted his little hands
and spoke his terrible language.
A billowing black smoke
poured forth
from his whole being,
lightning struck from within it ...

and crashed down into Bryony's
most perfect creation.

CHAPTER 12

All Hail

The King was entertaining guests
in the osseous dining hall,
licking his fingers
and laughing a fake laugh
whilst his guests guzzled
and guffawed,
their hands greasy from their
huge meat-filled feasts.
They heard it before they saw it,

a thumping,
a roaring,
a growling,
a clawing.

The Feather-Masked Guard
ran to The King's side,
blunderbuss in hand.
And that's when the walls crashed in
in huge toothy chunks,
as every animal that had ever been saved
by the prince, by Chain-Breaker Jack,
came crashing through the walls...

There were bears with bandages,

and lions with leprosy,

wolves with wounds,

toucans with tourniquets,

hawks with headaches

and chimps with limps.
And many, many more.

They moved as one,
an imposing force of scales,
of feathers and spines,
moving their many arms
and their many claws,
swishing their hundred tails,
cawing through a thousand beaks,
flapping in a flamboyance of wings.

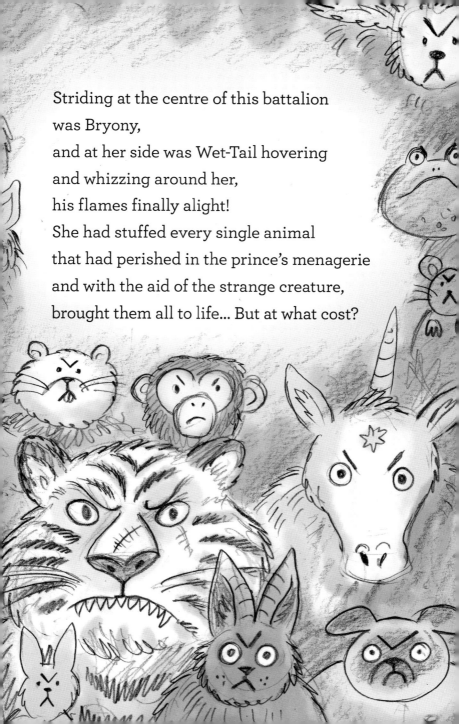

Striding at the centre of this battalion
was Bryony,
and at her side was Wet-Tail hovering
and whizzing around her,
his flames finally alight!
She had stuffed every single animal
that had perished in the prince's menagerie
and with the aid of the strange creature,
brought them all to life... But at what cost?

The King spat out his food in shock
as the animal brigade stalked towards him,
as all the animals remembered
their capture by trappers and fur merchants,
the suffering caused by The King's laws,
laws that misused and mistreated the
natural world.

The King was a blubbering mess,
terrified by the beasts that snarled and
hissed and barked at him.

"Miss Bryony – please don't hurt The King."

It was Yeltsin calling to her
from amid the rubble of the osseous hall.
Bryony could feel the heat and excitement
and anger rising up in her.
Her capture,
her imprisonment,
her days spent sewing and stuffing
animals that had been left to die,
the bargain with the strange little creature,
all rising up in her.
All these men
telling her what to do.
Now she had the upper hand
and she would take it...

"Please! Bryony ... show mercy,
The King has suffered enough."

This time it was The Feather-Masked Guard.
Bryony looked at the deflated king
and thought of the
prince in the casket.
She could not imagine the heartache
that The King must have felt.
But also, she could not see
how such a king could be at such odds
with his son, how such a man who cared
nothing for the natural world could rule
a kingdom.

*"Your majesty. I am relieving you
of your crown and making myself
queen of all."*
Yeltsin and The Feather-Masked Guard
were stunned.
The King blubbered loudly,
his sadness overtaking him.

There was a moment of silence
as Bryony took in the crowd
of The King's royal guests
and extended family.
They peered at her, mouths agape,
and she stared back,
daring them to challenge her,
daring them to question her.
Wet-Tail whizzed around them,
his flame alighting their shock.

"All hail, Queen Bryony,"
came Yeltsin's call.

"All hail, Queen Bryony,"
came the bellowing response
from The Feather-Masked Guard.

And just like that,
    like a wave,
    like a sigh of relief,
the many guests
took up the chant...

"All hail, Queen Bryony,
first of her name,
queen of death,
renewer of pets,
stitcher of many skins."

CHAPTER 13

Changing Times

News travelled far and wide
of the new queen and her terrible army.
(They were in fact just her animal friends.)
No one dared move against her
or threaten her people,
or her kingdom,
or her seat in power,
so powerful was the idea of her.

The catching of wild animals

                   was stopped!

The selling of furs

         banned!

Cruelty of any kind to animalkind

            severely punished.

The old king was well looked after
and given time to mourn his son.
He buried him out on the cliff-edged glade
where his menagerie ended,
and found a comfort
that slowly forged its way into his heart.

Bryony built her own palace
right in the centre of everything.
The new palace was unlike anything Mythica
had ever seen. It was park and mountain,
it was forest and lake,
ocean and glade with waterfalls
and treetop rooms
and space for all who needed it.
A place where animals lived
side by side with people.

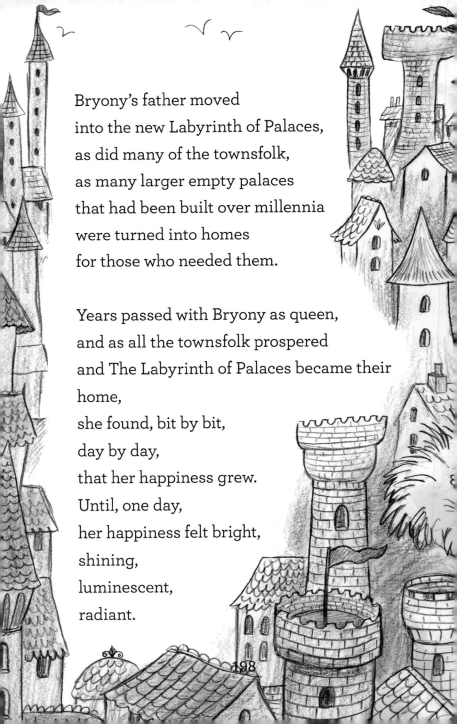

Bryony's father moved
into the new Labyrinth of Palaces,
as did many of the townsfolk,
as many larger empty palaces
that had been built over millennia
were turned into homes
for those who needed them.

Years passed with Bryony as queen,
and as all the townsfolk prospered
and The Labyrinth of Palaces became their
home,
she found, bit by bit,
day by day,
that her happiness grew.
Until, one day,
her happiness felt bright,
shining,
luminescent,
radiant.

And that was the day
the strange little creature came to call.

CHAPTER 14

Frankenstiltskin

On the day Bryony's happiness
became its most radiant,
a small round door
that wasn't there before
inched, creaked, then gaped open
in a wall of her plant-studded bedroom.
As she sat stroking
all her beasts of many skins,
the little creature appeared
with his mismatched eyes
and his patchwork face,
swishing his black curls
and smiling with his pearly white teeth.

"I have come to collect
my happiness, my pet,"

he drawled.

Bryony had spent years ruling.
She was far from the scared girl
that had been swiped
by a sad king
from her doting father's workshop.
She had been preparing for this moment.

"I don't wish to give you my happiness.
There must be another arrangement we can make."

The little creature was devious,
the little creature was magical,
and, like all magical beings,
it was bound by bargains
and tempted by gambles.

"If you can guess my name,
you can keep your happiness.
But if you cannot I shall...

Strip all the joy away from you.
Rip all the joy away from your palace.
Peel all the joy away from your kingdom.
And make it all my own.

You have three guesses,
and by the third guess
your entire kingdom
will be one of encyclopedic misery."

The memory of her Death-Dream,
of the bargain the prince had made
years before with this same creature,
flashed into her head.

"*Very well,*" she said.

"*But I wish to amend the game slightly.
To make it more interesting.
You will give me three guesses
but over three days.
And if by the third day
my answers are still incorrect,
you will win.*"

With the bargain amended
the little creature disappeared
through his little round door.

In her time as ruler of all of Mythica
Bryony had never let
anyone get the upper hand.
Her ordeal of being forced
to stuff animals for The King
was still fresh in her mind.
And whilst the creature
had helped her,
that was before she was a queen

      with responsibilities,

      with a kingdom,

      with people who depended on her,

      with a very full sock drawer.

She was not prepared
to bargain with the kingdom's happiness.

Bryony mounted Wet-Tail,
who had grown considerably over the years,
wearing her flame-proof riding armour.
She whispered sweetly into his large ears
and Wet-Tail exploded into flames ...
and lifted her up and out into her kingdom.

First, they flew east
over The Labyrinth of Palaces,
its winding streets now thrumming
with activity, laughter and life.

Bryony spotted her old home,
her father's old workshop,
in the old ramshackle hamlet
she knew so well,
where scaffolding and
new buildings were going up
in every direction,
where new parks and gardens
and forests were being planted
as the people and animals, all over,
flourished under her rule.

She landed at the furthest hamlet
to the east of her kingdom.
The children were the first to run to her,

awed by her friend Wet-Tail
and his dancing flame.
They laughed and giggled
as Wet-Tail zoomed around their village
and spat fire balls into the air
and extinguished his flames
so they could pet his head
and nuzzle his warm chin.
And soon their parents
and grandparents followed.
And once everyone was seated
and the fires were lit
and the hot chocolate passed around
and everyone was ready,
Queen Bryony told a story.

She spoke of her father
who was so proud of her
(perhaps too proud),
and their shop,
and the sad king,
and a prince who saved animals,
and their tragic end,
and her imprisonment,
and her taxidermy work,
and the little creature,
and his strange powers,
and left nothing out.
And when the children asked...

"What is the little creature's name?"

Queen Bryony replied...

"His name is Frankenstiltskin."

A name of her own choosing,
dreamt up in her own head,
told in her own story.

When she returned to her palace that night
the little creature appeared
through his little round door and said...

"What is my name, pet?"

"Your name is Frankenstiltskin."

The little creature laughed
a cruel slippery laugh.

"That is a ridiculous name,
and is no name of mine.
That is one guess gone,
you have two guesses left.
Do better tomorrow
or your happiness will be MINE!!!"

And with that he left
through his strange little door.
And Bryony felt a sadness creep
that she had never felt before.

The following morning
Queen Bryony mounted Wet-Tail
and this time flew west,
over deserts
and grassy steppes,
and landed in a hamlet
where the men and women
spun hay into gold.

As before, the children gathered first,
then their parents joined and their parents.
Queen Bryony told her story
and left nothing out.
And when they asked
the name of the strange little creature
with the criss-cross face and magical hands,
she said...

"His name is Frankenstiltskin."

That night the creature returned again,
his smile even crueller.

"What is my name, my pet?"

"Your name is Frankenstiltskin,"

insisted Queen Bryony,
and the little creature
near wept with laughter.

"Silly pet – you are no queen.
You said that name yesternight,
that was the worst guess I'd ever seen.
You have just one more chance to get it right!"

And with that he left
through his strange little door.
And from her palace she heard sad wails
that she had never heard before.

The following morning
Queen Bryony
was up early,
before the sun opened its eyes,
before the birds remembered to sing.

This time she flew north
on her great fire-drake,
over ice capped mountains,
and told her story.

She then flew south
as far as the purple sanded dunes
that embraced her kingdom,
and told her story.
And each time
when the people asked
about the name
of the strange little creature
with the patchwork face
and magical hands,
she replied...

"His name is Frankenstiltskin."

As she flew home to her palace
she could hear a thrum
in the kingdom below,
and her heart sank.

"Oh no, Wet-Tail,
I think sadness has found my kingdom."

But the thrum wasn't one of despondency,
or melancholy,
or even a little bleakness.
The thrum was one
of a good story,
nay not a good story,
a great story,
of magic and mischief,
of lost love
and new beginnings.

News travelled faster than she could fly,
of how Bryony had become queen,
of how she had stuffed and stitched
a whole menagerie
of wronged animals back together,
of how that menagerie was brought to life
by a strange little creature
with a mish-mashed face
and magical hands
by the name of Frankenstiltskin.

CHAPTER 15

The Power of a Word

The name Frankenstiltskin could be heard and seen everywhere around Mythica. It was in every newspaper...

On every billboard...

On the side of every bus...

His name was being spoken by every child
and every adult,
miaowed by every cat
and mooed by every duck
(those poor confused ducks),
until there wasn't a soul in Bryony's
kingdom
who did not know,
for a fact,
undeniably,
without a whiff of a doubt,
a shadow of a doubt,
a crumb
    a hum
        or a whisper of a doubt,

that the name of the creature was ...
                Frankenstiltskin.

That night,
the little round door
opened with less gusto,
less relish,
less bravado than before.
The strange little creature
flopped into Bryony's chamber,
his tail dragging behind him.

"What is my name?" he asked,
his frown pronounced,
his eyes dull and sad,
a little grey showing in his black curls,
a little rot stinking in his teeth,
his stitchings, itching.

Queen Bryony fixed him
with a royal stare
of queenly intent
and without hesitation,
resignation or consternation
told him...

Your name IS

Frankenstiltskin.

There was no laughter
from his cruel little mouth,
no dance in his cruel little eyes.

"You are truly a queen,
a ruler,
a storyteller.
My name is indeed now Frankenstiltskin,
for no one will call me by anything else,
no one sees me as anything else,
no one has heard of anyone else.
You have destroyed me with a word,
my queen."

As the little creature spoke,
Queen Bryony noticed
that the stitches that crisscrossed his face
started to glow,
started to unravel,

as the little creature
started to fall apart.
A pointed ear and blinking eye
falling to the left,
a clawed hand and a furry shoulder
falling to the right.
His legs crumpling beneath him
like a popped balloon.

All that was left
was a patchwork of furs
and the leathers of his skins
in an untidy pile on the ground.

Bryony called for her tongue
Yeltsin Thorogood
(who was far happier serving her than
the old king)
and for her Feather-Masked Guard
and for her doting father.
Bryony told them to gather the creature's
remains.

Queen Bryony tasked her taxidermist father
with the job of stuffing the creature,
mounting him
and presenting him
in her kingdom's grandest museum.
He had pride of place alongside the many displays
that Bryony and her father had created
over many years to educate and inform,
to comfort and astound.

FRANKENSTILTSKIN

People came from miles around
to see the display
and to remember that Bryony was queen,
not only because of her skill and ingenuity
and her pain and her bravery,
but also because of a little bit of magic
from a strange little creature
with a name gifted by a queen.
The name of ...

EPILOGUE

I hope you enjoyed
the true story of FRANKENSTILTSKIN
and the taxidermist, Queen Bryony.
Let's hope that Frankenstiltskin's new position
on display in the museum
is not too TAXING!!!

MUAHAHAHAHAHAHA!

I really must go. There is a whiff of a foul smell
coming from my bookcase of fairy tales
which can only mean one thing...
Some of the stories are starting to leak out!

I must grab my mop and bucket,
my gloves and my prodding sticks,
if I'm to get those trembling tales
back into their books.

I do hope you'll join me again soon,
for more ...

Fairy Tales Gone Bad!